DISNEY KINGDOMS
SEEKERS OF THE WEIRD
#3

When their parents were kidnapped by the sinister Shadow Society, Maxwell and Melody Keep followed their mysterious Uncle Roland through a portal to the Museum of the Weird, a vast depository of the world's most powerful—and threatening—supernatural objects.

While trying to retrieve a set of items needed to rescue the Keeps, Roland was seriously injured and tasked the sniping siblings with completing the mission. Now the teens must use the objects to obtain and hand over an infamous item known as the Coffin Clock to the Society before the creepy Candleman burns down—or they'll never see their parents again!

Facing a variety of the Museum's odd objects, from flying books to mummified Husks, Maxwell and Melody found the first object, the Walking Chair...but were then confronted by a group of ghostly Museum Wardens who delivered a dire warning: Stop what you're doing or doom the world!

MAXWELL KEEP
Brother

MELODY KEEP
Sister

ROLAND KEEP
Uncle, Warden

CANDLEMAN
Timekeeper

HEAD WARDEN

BRANDON SEIFERT writer   FILIPE ANDRADE artist
JEAN-FRANCOIS BEAULIEU colorist   VC'S JOE CARAMAGNA letterer

MICHAEL DEL MUNDO cover artist
BRIAN CROSBY variant cover artist

JIM CLARK, BRIAN CROSBY, TOM MORRIS
& JOSH SHIPLEY walt disney imagineers

MARK BASSO assistant editor   BILL ROSEMANN editor

AXEL ALONSO editor in chief   JOE QUESADA chief creative officer
DAN BUCKLEY publisher

special thanks to DAVID GABRIEL

MUSEUM OF THE WEIRD inspired by the designs of ROLLY CRUMP

 Spotlight

marvelkids.com

ABDOPUBLISHING.COM

Reinforced library bound edition published in 2017 by Spotlight, a division of ABDO, PO Box 398166, Minneapolis, Minnesota 55439. Spotlight produces high-quality reinforced library bound editions for schools and libraries. Published by agreement with Marvel Characters, Inc.

Printed in the United States of America, North Mankato, Minnesota.
042016
092016

 THIS BOOK CONTAINS RECYCLED MATERIALS

 marvelkids.com © 2014 MARVEL

Elements based on Walt Disney's Museum of the Weird © Disney.

PUBLISHER'S CATALOGING IN PUBLICATION DATA

Names: Seifert, Brandon, author. | Moline, Karl ; Magyar, Rick ; Beaulieu, Jean-Francois ; Andrade, Filipe, illustrators.

Title: Disney Kingdoms : Seekers of the weird / by Brandon Seifert ; illustrated by Karl Moline, Rick Magyar, Jean-Francois Beaulieu, and Filipe Andrade.

Description: Minneapolis, MN : Spotlight, [2017] | Series: Disney Kingdoms : seekers of the weird

Summary: When their parents are abducted, Melody and Maxwell Keep follow their estranged uncle Roland through a portal to the Museum of the Weird, and are thrust into a dangerous mission to save their family and the world from an evil shadow society!

Identifiers: LCCN 2016932365 | ISBN 9781614795148 (v.1 : lib. bdg.) | ISBN 9781614795155 (v. 2 : lib. bdg.) | ISBN 9781614795162 (v. 3 : lib. bdg.) | ISBN 9781614795179 (v. 4 : lib. bdg.) | ISBN 9781614795186 (v. 5 : lib. bdg.)

Subjects: LCSH: Disney (Fictitious characters)--Juvenile fiction. | Rescues--Juvenile fiction. | Museums--Juvenile fiction. | Adventure and adventurers--Juvenile fiction. | Comic books, strips, etc.--Juvenile fiction. | Graphic novels--Juvenile fiction.

Classification: DDC 741.5--dc23

LC record available at http://lccn.loc.gov/2016932365

ABDO

Spotlight

A Division of ABDO
abdopublishing.com

UNCLE ROLAND SAID THE MUSH-ROOM PEOPLE...

...ARE LIKE THE MUSEUM'S MAINTENANCE CREW, RIGHT?

SO WHY ARE THEY CHASING--

MAXWELL!

YOU ARE SO A.D.H.D. SOMETIMES!

WHAT ARE YOU EVEN--

OH. THINK HE WAS A WARDEN?

I GUESS, MELODY! HE'S WEARING THE RIGHT CLOTHES...

EVER SEE A DEAD PERSON BEFORE?

NO... ...I MEAN, IF THE HUSKS DON'T COUNT.

IS IT EVERYTHING YOU DREAMED IT WOULD BE?

YOU'RE STEALING FROM THE DEAD? THAT IS SO LIKE YOU.

HE'S PROBABLY GOING TO COME BACK AND HAUNT YOU OR SOMETHING.

MELODY, I'M NOT KEEPING IT! I JUST WANT TO LOOK.

I SWEAR I'VE SEEN THIS MEDALLION SOMEWHERE BEFORE...

...BESIDES ASK THEM *NOT* TO HURT US?

SERIOUSLY?

DON'T *HURT* US? *PLEASE?*

WE'RE JUST TRYING TO HELP OUR *PARENTS.* THEY'RE BEING HELD FOR *RANSOM!* MAYBE YOU GUYS *KNOW* THEM?

THEY'RE *WARDENS.* AND--

UH, MAYBE WE SHOULDN'T SAY THE "W" WORD?

WORKING FOR THE WARDENS REALLY *STINKS,* DOESN'T IT?

I BET THEY MAKE YOU DO LOTS OF STUFF YOU DON'T WANT TO *DO.*

AND MAKE YOU WORK WHEN YOU DON'T *WANT* TO WORK.

I BET YOU *HATE* IT.

HEHE HEHE HE...

WHAT'S SO FUNNY?

MY DEAR YOUNG LADY--

--I AM NO GHOST.

MY PHYSICAL BODY IS IN A TRANCE SOME DISTANCE AWAY, WHILE MY ETHERIC BODY VISITS YOU--

--TO DELIVER A DIRE WARNING.

"DIRE," HUH?

BUT NOT, YOU KNOW, SO DIRE YOU'D BOTHER TO DELIVER IT IN THE FLESH?

IT'S IMPOSSIBLE AT PRESENT FOR THE OTHER WARDENS AND ME TO ACCESS THE MUSEUM--

--AS YOUR UNCLE STOLE ALL OUR KEYS.

YOU CAN'T TRUST ROLAND. HE'S TRYING TO DELIVER THE COFFIN CLOCK TO DESPOINA AND HER SHADOW SOCIETY!

YOU-- YOU WANT US TO JUST TAKE YOUR WORD FOR IT?

WHO ARE YOU?

EFRAIN FENTON WHETSTONE-- CHIEF WARDEN. YOUR PARENTS' EMPLOYER.

WHAT DID ROLAND TELL YOU OF THE COFFIN CLOCK?

HE TOLD US IT'S--

--WELL, THAT IT'S IMPORTANT, AND...

DID HE TELL YOU IT'S NOT SIMPLY SHAPED LIKE A COFFIN--IT IS A COFFIN?

OR MORE ACCURATELY, A PRISON CELL...

...AFTER THE REAPER KING CLEARS IT OF ALL *LIVING* PEOPLE.

...

LAST TIME HE WAS FREE, THE REAPER KING KILLED A *THIRD* OF EUROPE.

NOW DO YOU UNDERSTAND THE *DANGER* YOU'RE PUTTING US ALL IN BY SEEKING THE CLOCK?

WHAT CAN WE *DO*?

YOU HAVE TO GIVE UP YOUR *QUEST*. LEAVE THE *COFFIN* WHERE IT LIES.

THE WARDENS CAN *PROTECT* YOU FROM DESPOINA.

YOU'RE ASKING US TO LEAVE OUR *PARENTS* TO *DIE*?

I'M *SORRY* ABOUT ARTHUR AND ELLEN...

...BUT I'M ASKING YOU NOT TO HELP DESPOINA *KILL MILLIONS* OF PEOPLE.

THAT'S... *NOT* GOING TO HAPPEN.

HOW CAN YOU BE SO *SURE*?

BECAUSE--

--WE AREN'T GOING TO *LET* IT.

SHAME. BUT I *DO* UNDERSTAND.

I GUESS THERE'S NOTHING TO BE *DONE* FOR IT, THEN.

IT...

...WORKED?

MAXWELL! THAT--

--THAT *DIDN'T ACTUALLY STINK!* CONGRATULATIONS!

WHAT ARE YOU DOING? DON'T STOP!

GET THEM!

NO! NO! STOP AGAIN!

YOU THINK I'M GOING TO LET IT *COME TO THAT*? WE *NEED* THE COFFIN CLOCK...

...SO WE CAN CONVINCE *DESPOINA* WE'RE GOING TO DO HER *INSANE PRISONER EXCHANGE.* WE *HAVE* TO, TO GET *CLOSE ENOUGH*--

TO *RESCUE MOM AND DAD*?

OBVIOUSLY. IT'S A *SHELL GAME*--THAT'S ALL.

IF THAT'S *ALL*--THEN WHY DIDN'T YOU *TELL* US THAT IN THE FIRST PLACE?

BECAUSE...

WE KEPT *ASKING* WHAT THE DEAL WAS WITH DESPOINA AND THE CLOCK! WHY NOT JUST *TELL* US?

...THEN YOU WOULD'VE *WORRIED.*

YOU WOULD'VE SPENT THIS WHOLE WEEK AFRAID YOU WERE DOING THE *WRONG* THING.

SO?

SO, I--I...

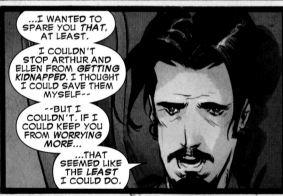

...I WANTED TO *SPARE* YOU *THAT,* AT LEAST.

I *COULDN'T* STOP ARTHUR AND ELLEN FROM *GETTING KIDNAPPED.* I THOUGHT I COULD SAVE THEM *MYSELF*--

--BUT I *COULDN'T.* IF I COULD KEEP YOU FROM *WORRYING MORE*--

...THAT SEEMED LIKE THE *LEAST* I COULD DO.

CAN I GET YOU TO *TRUST ME* AGAIN?

IT'S NOT GOING TO BE *EASY,* BUDDY.

TO *BEGIN* WITH-- HOW ABOUT ACTING LIKE YOU TRUST *US*?

HMM. IN *THAT* CASE...

...WHAT IF I *BUY* YOUR *TRUST*?

TO BE CONTINUED!

Disney Kingdoms: Seekers of the Weird #3 — Variant Cover by Brian Crosby

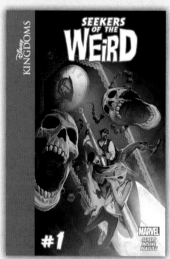

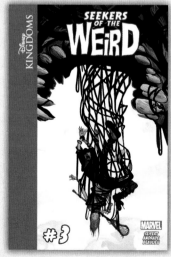

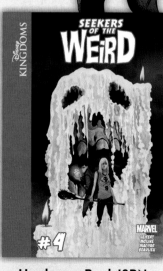